Dear Parents:

Congratulations! Your child is taking the first steps on an exciting journey. The destination? Independent reading!

STEP INTO READING® will help your child get there. The program offers five steps to reading success. Each step includes fun stories and colorful art or photographs. In addition to original fiction and books with favorite characters, there are Step into Reading Non-Fiction Readers, Phonics Readers and Boxed Sets, Sticker Readers, and Comic Readers—a complete literacy program with something to interest every child.

Learning to Read, Step by Step!

Ready to Read   Preschool–Kindergarten
• big type and easy words • rhyme and rhythm • picture clues
For children who know the alphabet and are eager to begin reading.

Reading with Help   Preschool–Grade 1
• basic vocabulary • short sentences • simple stories
For children who recognize familiar words and sound out new words with help.

Reading on Your Own   Grades 1–3
• engaging characters • easy-to-follow plots • popular topics
For children who are ready to read on their own.

Reading Paragraphs   Grades 2–3
• challenging vocabulary • short paragraphs • exciting stories
For newly independent readers who read simple sentences with confidence.

Ready for Chapters   Grades 2–4
• chapters • longer paragraphs • full-color art
For children who want to take the plunge into chapter books but still like colorful pictures.

STEP INTO READING® is designed to give every child a successful reading experience. The grade levels are only guides; children will progress through the steps at their own speed, developing confidence in their reading. The F&P Text Level on the back cover serves as another tool to help you choose the right book for your child.

Remember, a lifetime love of reading starts with a single step!

Visit us on the Web!
StepIntoReading.com
randomhousekids.com

Educators and librarians, for a variety of teaching tools, visit us at
RHTeachersLibrarians.com

Library of Congress Cataloging-in-Publication Data is available upon request.
ISBN 978-0-553-53896-0 (trade) — ISBN 978-0-553-53897-7 (lib. bdg.) — 978-0-553-53898-4 (ebook)

Printed in the United States of America
10 9 8 7 6 5 4 3 2 1

This book has been officially leveled by using the F&P Text Level Gradient™ Leveling System.

STEP INTO READING®

1
STEP
READY TO READ

Mama Loves

by Molly Goode

illustrated by Lisa McCue

Random House 🏠 New York

Mama loves
her little one.
She stays with him
night and day.

When her little one
gets hot,
she shoots
a cooling spray.

Mama teaches cub
to fish
in rivers fast
and wide.

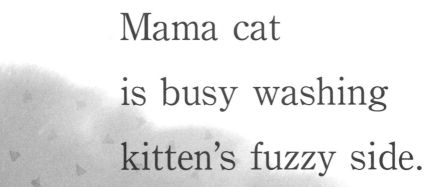

Mama cat
is busy washing
kitten's fuzzy side.

Mama loves her
little calf.

She helps her
to breathe air.

Baby panda's
never sad,
for Mama's
always there.

Mama otter
wants to show
her baby
how to swim.
Baby otter
loves to play . . .

14

. . . and lets Mama
push him in!

Ducklings,
one, two, three,
and four,
have webby
little feet.

Mama takes them
on a walk.
They line up
nice and neat.

Mama's brand-new
little one
drinks milk
to grow so tall!

Mama robin
watches baby
so she will not
slip and fall.

Mama minds her
little cubs
as they roll
and play.

They are learning
tricks to help them
hunt for food
one day.

Mama loves
her baby so.
She likes to
watch him splash.

If ever
there is danger,
she will help him
in a flash.

Hold on,
little koala!
Ride on
Mama's back.

She climbs
a leafy tree
to get you both
a yummy snack.

Mama keeps
her joey safe
inside her pouch
so snug.

Mama flies

into the night,

then flies back
to give a hug.

Holding, sharing,
teaching, caring,
mamas watch
you grow.

Duckling, fawn,
pup, kit,
or kitten . . .

. . . mamas love
you so!